Hello, Mr World

To my grandchildren

Sam, Chloe, Scout and Poppy

First published 2017 by Walker Books Ltd, 87 Vauxhall Walk, London SE11 5HJ

2 4 6 8 10 9 7 5 3 1

© 2017 Michael Foreman

The right of Michael Foreman to be identified as author/illustrator of this work has been
asserted by him in accordance with the Copyright, Designs and Patents Act 1988

This book has been typeset in JournalText

Printed in China

British Library Cataloguing in Publication Data:
a catalogue record for this book is available from the British Library

ISBN 978-1-4063-6657-0

www.walker.co.uk

Hello, Mr World

Michael Foreman

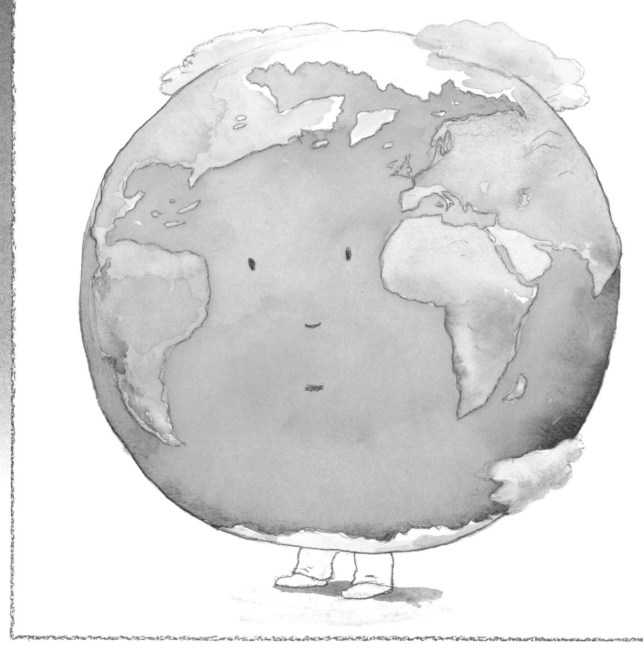

WALKER BOOKS

AND SUBSIDIARIES

LONDON • BOSTON • SYDNEY • AUCKLAND

"Today let's be doctors!"

"Hello, Mr World. How are you today?"

"Not good. I don't feel well."

"Oh dear, we're sorry to hear that. Please take a seat. Now, what seems to be the matter?"

"I keep getting hot and sweaty,
and I find it hard to breathe."

"Let's check your temperature.
Oh, you *are* much too hot. Hop onto
the bed please, Mr World, and
we'll have a closer look."

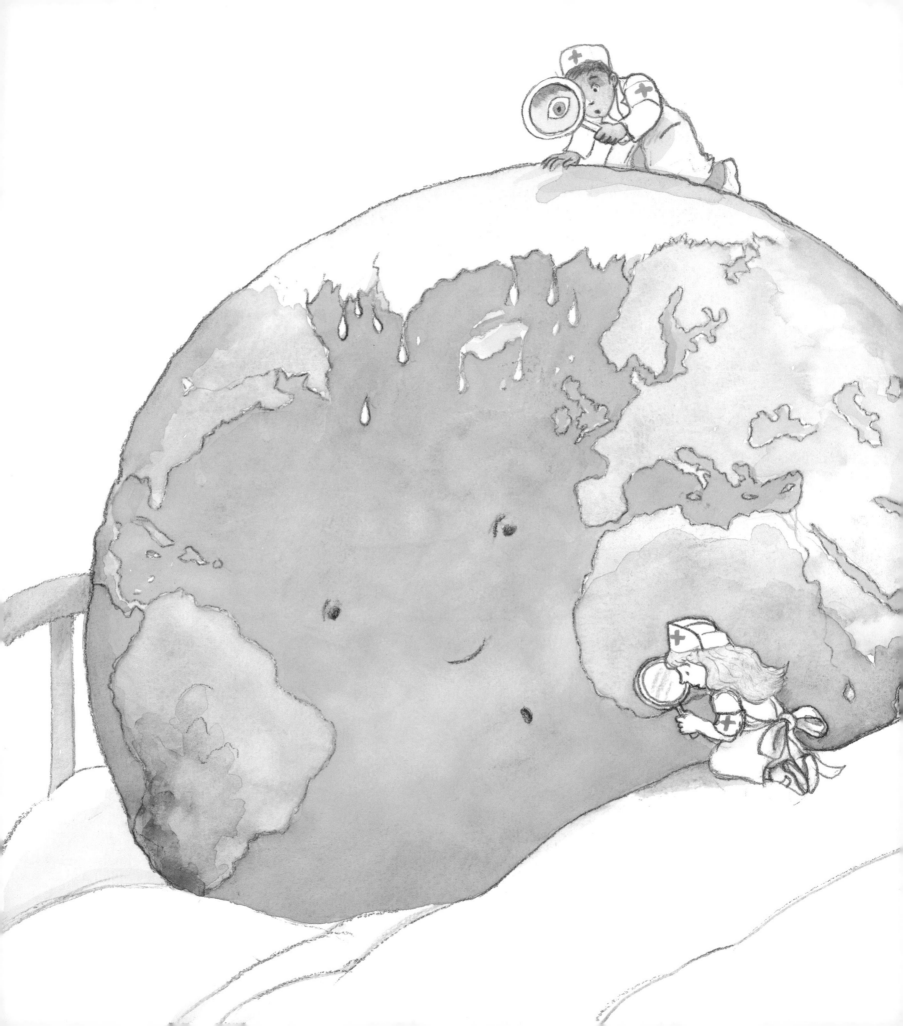

"Now we can see the problem. You're too hot up here, where you should be nice and cold, so your lovely snowy parts are melting—"

"And you're wet and sweaty over here. Let's have a closer look."

"The poor animals are in danger."

"They'll have nowhere to live."

"What else is wrong?"

"I cough a lot."

"Oh, poor Mr World.
Let's listen to your chest.
Your breathing doesn't
sound good."

"We need to take an X-ray.
Just relax and lie very still."

"Let's have a closer look."

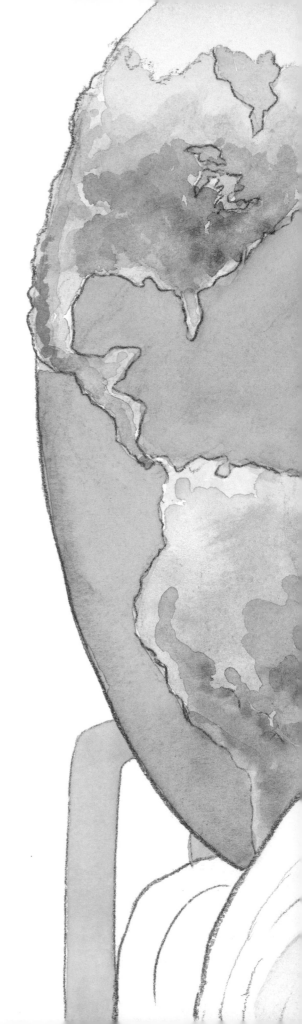

"Oh dear, you're full of smoke and fumes.
That's what makes you hot and breathless."

"You can't go on like this, Mr World. You must look to the future or things will just get worse..."

"What can I do to make it better?"

"Well, think of all the wonderful things you have, and how you can take care of them."

"I don't think I can do that on my own. Will you help me?"

"Yes, we will!"

"And we will too!
We are the future,
Mr World,

AND WE WILL
LOOK AFTER YOU."

Climate Change

In this story Mr World feels hot and sweaty.
In real life the world is getting hotter too.

We call this *climate change*.

The main thing that makes the world too hot is a gas. It exists in the air around us. The gas is made when we burn oil and coal in cars and aeroplanes and factories and power stations. Too much of this gas harms the world.

Trees and other plants use up this gas when they grow. They help keep the world nice and cool. But people are cutting down big forests, to make space for other things. So less of the gas is being used up.

Lots of animals are losing their homes as the world get warmer. People are worried that some, like polar bears and tigers, will disappear altogether.

All of these things are happening all the time, and the world keeps getting hotter.

But *you* can help!

Turning off lights, saving water when you clean your teeth and walking or biking (instead of going in a car) are some of the ways you can help the world and its animals. This is because when you switch on a light or turn on a tap or drive in a car, you are using energy. Most of the energy comes from the power stations that send out the gas that is warming up the world. If you use less energy then less gas will be made. And the more people who do this, the better. So, the best thing you can do is to persuade a friend, or two, to help as well!